担子

[上册]

Carrying Load

高山 著

担子
你挑起了希望
你挑满了善良
挑战了人生
挑明了道路
挑起了家的栋梁
挑选了心的模样

作家出版社

图书在版编目（CIP）数据

担子 / 高山 著. -- 北京 : 作家出版社，2015. 9
ISBN 978-7-5063-8308-0

Ⅰ. ①担… Ⅱ. ①高… Ⅲ. ①诗集 - 中国 - 当代
Ⅳ. ①I227

中国版本图书馆CIP数据核字（2015）第224919号

担　子

作　　者： 高　山
责任编辑： 贺　平
装帧设计： 萨福诗歌作坊
出版发行： 作家出版社
社　　址： 北京农展馆南里10号　　**邮　　编：** 100125
电话传真： 86-10-65930756（出版发行部）
86-10-65004079（总编室）
86-10-65015116（邮购部）
E-mail:zuojia@zuojia.net.cn
http://www.haozuojia.com（作家在线）
印　　刷： 广州星河印刷有限公司
成品尺寸： 150 × 240
字　　数： 60千
印　　张： 29.5（全二册）
版　　次： 2015年12月第1版
印　　次： 2015年12月第1次印刷
ISBN 978-7-5063-8308-0
定　　价： 38. 00元（全二册）

向更高的存在攀登

——序诗人高山诗集《担子》

谯达摩

认识广东诗人高山，是因为诗歌结的缘。2014 年，我担任团中央《中华儿女》杂志社海外版 4 月份的专刊主编，在大量来稿中，我发现高山的诗非常有生活气息，非常接地气，非常有个性。俄罗斯诗人巴尔蒙特曾说过：“个性的最大原则在于从群体中脱身，分离，逃开。”诗人高山的诗，主要挖掘自己的童年记忆和内心世界，小时候的点点滴滴的乡村生活不断地渗透到他的诗篇之中，不断地构建自己独特的艺术个性，不断地形成和丰富当下中国的一个优秀诗人——高山。

广东地处中国的南端，那里是最近 30 多年中国改革开放和市场经济建设的最前沿。最近 30 年来，广东省出了不少诗人，高山是其中的优秀一员。用诗人高山的话来说，他与诗歌互相拥抱，相互融为一体。他说：“我写诗歌，诗歌写我，愿诗与我同行，与自然同行，与时间和沧桑同行。诗是人的天性，如果用心观察，每个人都是诗人，每天都充满诗意，世界本来就是诗！”以高山为代表，广东诗人群一直在坚持诗歌写作、诗歌探索和诗歌实践，并始终坚守诗歌这块神圣的阵地，迄今为止，取得了令人瞩目的创作成就。

我担任主编的《中华儿女》杂志社海外版专刊发表了诗人高山的3首诗：《梦中梨花地》，《担子》，《绿荫下的女子》。这3首诗，可以看作是诗人高山的创作审美取向：诗的象征性审美取向，从而区别于当下中国诗坛无处不在的“口语化”写作。我认为，新诗要用充满着暗示的、能够引发预感的声音说话；在新诗中，应当自由而有机地融合两个内容：隐秘的抽象性和显明的意向美。高山的诗《梦中梨花地》、《担子》和《绿荫下的女子》均涵纳了直接的、具体的内容与丰富的色彩微差，那种用最纤细温柔的线与具体内容保持有机联系的潜在内容，并且这内容在一定程度上总是自在之物，自主地存在之物。因此，当广东诗人高山以《担子》一诗的标题作为他即将出版的诗集的书名，就显得意味深长，而且非常具有现代性象征性意义。高山在其以《担子》为题的那首诗中向我们展示了诗人的童年生活：“小时候／偏僻的农村／弯弯曲曲的羊肠草道／一望无际金灿灿稻田／／凶猛的水牛边／脆弱的我／单薄的肩膀上、挑着／一副晃悠悠担子／／左边是鸡／右边是鸭／绒毛松散叽叽喳喳／嗷嗷待哺”，并庄严地宣称：“担子／可爱又深沉的担子／我愿一生／把你形影不离的挑在肩上／与你并肩作战”。

诗人高山在这里以其生花妙笔，绘出了中国南方乡村绚丽多彩的场景。透过这种对南方乡村场景的精细描绘，《担子》揭示出：大自然拥有自己生生不息永恒交替的生命周期，宇宙万物兴衰枯荣均恪守各自独特的机制。写景、抒情与哲理自然交融，浑为一体。高山的诗句与他的世界观是严整和质朴的，这一点非常可贵，从某种意义上又使他的诗歌作品显得非常富有艺术价值。是的，高山的诗写的新颖、响亮，有一种童稚般纯洁的东西，也有一种对大自然的敏锐嗅觉。不久，诗人高山告别了自己的童年，开始体验生活所赋予的坎坷与艰辛："长大了 / 郊区的小城 / 零零散散三三二二的人群 / 时走时停忽左忽右的篷车 // 灼热的水泥马路上 / 年少的我 / 柔软的肩膀上、挑着 / 一副硬绑绑担子 // 前面是米 / 后面是书 / 摇摇欲坠叮叮咚咚 / 艰难前行"。

这些诗句，看上去非常写实，但放在整首《担子》里，则显得非常厚重。无论是"时走时停忽左忽右的篷车"，还是"一副硬绑绑担子"，都深深传达着诗人真挚、敏感、多情的心弦，使其发出动人、含蓄、优美的旋律，把人们带到一个"生命中不可承受之轻"的属于娑婆世界的众苦交煎的境界。漂泊、磨练之后，诗人进城参加工作了，诗人写道："后来 / 工作了 / 诺大的城市 / 熙熙攘攘红红绿绿的男女 / 来来往往黄黄白白的轿车 // 宽广的柏油马路上 / 成年的我 / 结实的肩膀上、挑着 / 一副无形的担子 // 这边是兄妹 / 那边是单位 / 踏踏实实规规矩矩 / 一丝不苟"。诗人即使进城参加工作了，但肩膀上的担子依旧没有任何减轻，依旧需要诗人继续在人生的道路上跋涉。细细品味这些诗句，诗人试图通过层层"意象"的转换，甚至是别出心裁的构思，现实景物与想象景物的复合，产生出一系列朴素的视觉意象。正是这种朴素的意象，涵纳着诗人的内在情思。透过诸如此类的意象对视觉美的呈现和内在情思的交融，构成了诗人高山诗歌作品所独具的审美效果。生活在继续，诗人的阅历在积累，在丰富。诗人接着写道："再后来／成功了／花花绿绿的大世界／各种各样皮肤东南西北的方言／宏观微观经济古今中外的思想／／人生感悟道路上／成熟的我／深沉的肩膀上、挑着／一副梦寐以求的担子／／左边是追求／右边是奉献／如履薄冰小心翼翼／无怨无悔"。

至此，诗人之思，诗之思，越来越澄明，越来越抵达"担子"的本真境界："担子／肩膀上的担子／越来越重却又／越来越轻／／担子／牵挂的担子／越来越远却又／越来越近／／担子／你挑起了希望／你挑满了善良／挑战了人生／挑明了道路／挑起了家的栋梁／挑选了心的模样／／担子／可爱又深沉的担子／我愿一生／把你形影不离的挑在肩上／与你并肩作战"。自然，这种诗之神韵、诗之品质的生成，应归功于南方乡村生活和都市生活的双重哺育，应归功于中国南方优秀诗人对大自然的那种特别锐敏而精细的审美感受力。那种审美感受力，使诗人高山能把南方钟灵毓秀的山山水水的灵魂逐步逐步地领悟，从而一步一步地把"担子"的哲学内涵向我们一点一点言说出来。正是在这个意义上，与其说高山是一个优秀诗人，倒不如说造化特意为了诗歌，为了表达人生无穷无尽的责任与使命，为了表达对中国南方乡村生活和都市生活的双重的爱和恻隐之心。

是的，诗歌艺术之神始终在人间行走，从来没有消失过，也绝对不会从人类的文化视野里消失。从古到今，从东方到西方，诗人及其作品都始终处于人类文明的核心部分，是人类永恒的精神家园。

是的，真正的诗人是不朽的。当中国新诗的发展历程进入 21 世纪，中国诗人们的创作激情几乎被市场经济的浪潮全部淹没。在此文化多元化的境遇下，诗歌不再像 20 世纪 80 年代、甚至 90 年代那样成为文化的中心和焦点，但诗人们仍然在思索，在写作，在探索真理。因此，我在此要衷心祝贺广东诗人高山的诗集《担子》出版问世。

2015 年 8 月 20 日，写于北京金泉广场

谯达摩简介：中央美术学院教授、北京大学文化产业委员会名誉主席、孔子和平奖评审委员会主席、《第三条道路》诗派创始人。

Reach For Higher Altitude

Preface for Gao Shan's collection Load Carrier

By Gautama

Igotto know Gao Shan the poet from Guangdong because of poetry. I was chief editor of the April special issue of China Profiles overseas version in 2014 and from the numerous ccontributions I found his poems, which are so true to life and special. As the Russian poet альмонт Константин Дмитриевич once said, "the nature of individuality lies in separation and isolation from the crow." Gao Shan's poems mainly focus on exploring into his childhood and inner world, the life details in the countryside constantly appear in his poems, which help establish his unique artistic personality and developing into and fulfilling him as an excellent contemporaty poet in China.

Guangdong province is located in the southern part of China and has been the poineer in reform and open–up of market–oriented economy construction the past 30 years. Quite a few excellent poets emerge in recently and one of them is Gao Shan. Just as he said, he and poems embrace each other and unite as one. " I write poems, poems write me, I wish to be with along with poems and nature, with time and change of the world. Poetry lies in human nature and with heart felt observation, everyone ca n be a poet and every day can be full of poetry. The world itself can be a poem." Poets in Guangdong province have been writing poems and studying into poems guarding this holy land with praise worthy achievements.

I had three of his poems published in the special issue of China Profiles overseas version, Pear Blossoms in My Dream, Carrying Load and A Young Girl in the Shade of Trees , which can be considered as his aesthetic inclination: the symbolic aesthetic inclination of his poems different from the colloquail tendency prevailing in the present Chinese poetic circles. I hold the belief that modern poems should be full of metaphors with the voice of a prophet, which should combine organically mystical abstraction and explict images. The three poems mentioned above all contain direct and concrete stories and different colors, connecting all the poetential contents with a delicate thread. In the meantime, all the contents exist in some extent by themselves. Therefore, the choice of name of this collection Load Carrier is of profound significance and modern symbolic sense. Carrying Load speads a vivid scene of his life as a child.

My childhood
At a remote village
Dirt paths winding
Golden wheat fields endless
How weal I was
By side of a strong buffalo
A load swinging
On my bony shoulders

A chicken on the left
A duck on the right
Furry feathers loosened
Chirping and chattering
Dying for food

And then he expresses his dertermination

Load
Lovely and deep
I am willing to carry you all my life
Fight my way on
Side by side

With these detailed descrptions, country life in southern China appears before our eyes. Carrying Load conveys the concept that nature has its own life pattern in endless succession and all things in the universe abide by their special mechanism of thriving and whithering, rising and declining. A natual fusion of feelings and settings and philosophical perspectives as one unity. Both his poems and his world view are serious and simple and unaffected, which in some sense adds to the artistic value to his poems. His poems are fresh and bright with purity and acute sensitivity to nature. Later on, he said goodbye to his childhood and started experiencing all the hardships and adversities in life:

Growing older
At a small town
A crowd of people
Walking stop and go
With overloaded trucks driving by

The cement road burning hot
Young as I was
Carrying a hard load
On my soft shoulder

Rice in the front

Books at the back

Shaking   stumbling

Struggling my way forward

All these verses appear realistic but prove to be profound in meaning in the whole poem. Whether overloaded trucks driving by or a hard load

Both produce touching as well as underlying melody with sincere ,sensitive and affectionate heart strings, bring the readers into a whirling world of minggled sufferings with The Unbearable Lightness of Being。 After wandering and going through hardships in life, he went to work in the city, when he wrote:

Later

I worked in a big city

Noisy with all walks of people   red and green

Busy with all kinds of cars   yellow and white

On a wide asphalt road

I was an adult

Strong shoulders

Carrying shapeless load

Brothers this side

Duty and work that side

With my footsteps steadyfast

Orderly and carefully

Although working in the city, the loads on his shoulders were still heavy and he continued struggling on his road in life.Chewing thsese verses, it is not difficult to find with the shifting of different layers of images and extraordinary plots,he intends to creat a series of plain visual scenes by blending the images in reality and those in imagination,all of which contribute to his special aesthetic effect of images and affections.As life went on, he bacame more experienced and he shared his what he went through :

Still later

With my dream achieved

In a bigger world

Meet people of all colors and different languages

Thinking about economy   macro and micro

Reflecting the past and the present   the Chinese and the western

On the road of life

I am now mature

With my dream load

On my tough shoulders

Pursuit on the left
Dedication on the right
Walk with caution as if on thin ice
But without regrets

Up till now, thoughts of the poet, thoughts of the poems have become

clearer and clearer and closer to the essence of Load Carrier.

Load
On my shoulders
Heavier and heavier
At the same time
Lighter and lighter
Load
Of concern
Farther and farther
Yet nearer and nearer

From load
I learn about
Hope

Kindness

Challenge in life

Way ahead

With a family to support

With a role model to follow

Load

Lovely and deep

I am willing to carry you all my life

Fight my way on

Side by side

There is no doubt that the development of such charm and nature of poetry can be separated from his growth in the countryside and the city owing to the delicate sensiblity in nature of a poet in southern China.

It' s this very sensiblity that enables Gao Shan to gradually understand the depths of the beautiful landscapes in the south, from which he exposes bit by bit the true essence of Load Carrier to us.So in this sense, rather than an excellent poet, Gao Shan is more of a heart and soul created by nature for poetry to carry out the endless duties and missions and convey the love and sympathy both for the country and the city life in southern China.

Truthly, muse is forever walking in human world and

constantly exist in our culture sight. Whether in ancient or modern times, western or eartern world, poets and their works lie in the core of human civiliation considered as the spiritual hometown of mankind.

True poets are immortal. As Chinese new poetry develops in the 21st century, passion for creation of Chinese poets nearly get submerged in the waves of market-oriented economy . In such multicultual world, poetry is no longer the center and focus of culture as in the 1980s and early 1990s. However, our poets never stop thinking and writing and exploring truth. So I would like to congratulate on the publication of Gao San' s collection of poems Load Carrier.

Aug,20, 2015

At Jinquan Plaza , Beijing

Gautama

Professor of China Central Academy Of Fine Arts;

Honeray president of Cultural Industry Committee of Beijing University;

Chairperson of Confucius Peace Award Committee;

Founder of the poetry school The Thrid Path

目录 CONTENTS

担子

上册

古诗

秋教

身隐群书日日忙
夜来休认镜中妆
邻家公子因国学
隔壁先生是酒狂
短鬓修脸逗童乐
红袖柳腰染清霜
秋鸣不时入人耳
拍手叫绝笑路傍

2014 年秋

Teaching in Autumn

Hidden in piles of books occupied day after day
Hardly recognize myself in the mirror at night
Neighboring young man learns Chinese classics
The Next door teacher is an alcohol addict
Short hair and thin face often laughed by the kids
Red sleeves willow waist and frost-like hair
Singing of autumn insects comes now and then
Clap and say Bravo happily by the roadside

Autumn 2014

秋 影

时光叠叠复重重
仿佛迷离梦幻中
身隔天涯无远近
心思明月锁玲珑
秋寒菊影魂应驻
霜冻传神梦也空
珍重泼成千点墨
谁家乖女醉朦胧

2014年秋

Autumn Impression

Hours overlap as if repeating itself
I am wandering in a misted illusion
Separated from each other far or near
Exquisite heart resembles the bright moon
Frost freezes messages   dream left void
Concern splashes ink   a thousand dots
Whose daughter drunk like the hazy moon

Autumn 2014

离母校二十六年有感

昔日离校今妪翁
建家立业人人同
女觅潘安男追月
两眼发光脸通红
见得金银闪闪亮
不顾一切收囊中
逐名求利累半死
落得荒名半癫疯
朝起暮回杯中酒
奈何饥肠轰隆隆
小富由勤大已定
不必逢人喊叫穷
三五知已亦可醉
孤男寡妇恨相逢
仁义礼德孝父母
且行且乐刚如松
休怨世间高低事
原来一切冥冥中

2015 年春

26 Years after Graduation

Left motherschool young and now old
Everyone the same with family and career
Seek guys handsome like Pan An or chase beauty like the moon
Faces flush with both eyes glaring
Light up at the sight of gold and silver
Take into the pocket without thinking
Pursue fame and profit tiring oneself to death
Reduced to reclaim and half insanity
From dawn till dusk drowned in wine
Yet stomach still rumbles like thunders
Wealth builds up with hard work as destined
No need to complain to whoever you meet
A few bosom friends are quite enough
Bachelor and widow find it late to meet
Benevolence righteousness propriety filial piety to parents
Enjoy life with an open mind and will upright like pine trees
Ignore affairs in the world whether high or low
Believing that all is defined by fate already

Spring 2015

忆往昔峥嵘岁月

昔日黄昏香满树
春男秋女花前踱
娥眉轻锁百媚顾
气宇慢昂千船渡
粗茶淡饭饥肠辘
晨光暮霭走自路
三更锣鸣五更鼓
更见先生把人数
借问麦哥是何木
敢教崔师显绝术
但使黄老丞相肚
不教书童满腹苦
二十六年残和酷
毕竟今日顶梁柱
曾经拈文又从武
不曾烟酒不曾赌
弄笔挥毫把诗煮
且当商人且当主
半生风流多感触
见惯峥嵘不屑怒
轻问来年君何处

On The Years of Struggles

Dusk in the past fragrant flowers covering the trees
People young and old wandered admiring the flowers
Willow leaf eyebrows frowning cast a hundred looks
Dignified and noble bearing welcome a thousand boats
Led a simple life with the stomach rumbling in hunger
For many dawns and dusks everyone on their own paths
Gong sound at three and drum beat at five o'clock
Then the teacher would have roll call one by one
Wondering who this Brother Mai might be that would
Dare to invite Master Cui to show his super Gong Fu
Persuade the school of Emperor Huang and Lao Tzu
To relieve the heavy study load of the young students
Hardship and torture throughout twenty six years
Has finally produced the present pillars of the state
Once I was adept with both the pen and the sword
Never smoked or drank nor was I addicted to gambling
But devoted to weighing and measuring the word
Both a merchant and bread winner of the family
Unrestrained for half of the life with complex feelings
Constantly witness different affairs with peaceful mind
If you ask where I will be in the years to go

高山常驻西南浦
暂假羊年思故土
梦得桃花千万亩
自古英雄美人故
唐朝兵马今陈墓
愿君深修把禅悟
爱国爱家爱父母
峥嵘岁月已尽数
不添遗憾不添堵
但愿良朋千万户
从此诗人不孤独

2015 年春

Surely it is the south west of our motherland
Miss my hometown at the start of the year of goat
Dream of peach blossoms over ten thousand miles
Since ancient times heroes are attached to beauties
Troops in Tang Dynasty now rest in the symmetry
Wish you mediate and understand the Buddhism
Love our motherland our family and parents
With the years of struggles approaching an end
Without regrets or troubles to disturb our minds
Wishing to have trustworthy friends over the world
Then I will never be left in solitary from now on

By Gao Shan

黄花记－三字文

老黄花，是一家
你揉面，我切瓜
老与少，乐哈哈
男与女，顶呱呱
朝上九，晚下五
一进门，把饭煮
夫去皮，妇剥骨
恩与爱，乐与苦
遵法纪，守行规
除邪恶，耀光辉
出师捷，凯旋归
淡名利，忘欢悲
三五朋，酒斟杯
莫道白，莫道黑
恩与怨，莫记怀
老同事，新秀才
离群马，发点财
勤劳富，牡丹栽
三羊泰，好运来
你我他，百花开
举琼浆，上高台
悲伤意，风雨埋

On Old Yellow Flower- Three Character Verse

Old Yellow Flower　my dear family

You make dough　I cut gourd

Old or young　fun and pleasure

Man and woman　perfect pair work

Start work at nine　finish at five

On returning home　start cooking meal

Husband skin chicken　wife cut bones

Gratitude and love　sorrow and joy

Obey the law　observe the regulation

Remove the evil　praise the glory

Achieve good grades　come back honored

Indifferent to fame　content with happiness

Argue not right　argue not wrong

Gratitude and resentment　neither matters much

Old work mates　new learned scholar

Leave the team　make some fortune

Build up wealth　marry the beauty

Peace and luck　meet good chances

He You and Me　blossoms in bloom

Raise good wine　ascend high platform

Sand and regret　wind and rain

你一言，我一语
陈新事，乐无比
虽天涯，千万里
若有情，聚一起
二十年，一瞬间
常牵挂，夜难眠
十三日，梦寐天
愿一切，皆成圆
不遗憾，不存嫌
高山言，落笔尖
愿大家，把喜添
情比铁，意更坚
思互感，梦相连
和与睦，倍温馨
诗将尽，汗已淋
忆往昔，泪满襟
莫仇富，莫笑贫
和与谐，甚比金
从此后，相见频
增友爱，互赞勤
闲暇事，莫管它
老黄花，是一家
男与女，乐哈哈
老与少，顶呱呱

2015 年春

此诗赠送老黄花全体同仁
预祝三月十三日聚会圆满成功

You said this I said that
Chatted about things glad beyond comparison
End of the world thousands of miles
Care and concern gather and reunite
Twenty years passed in one instant
Miss you constantly hard to sleep
Thirteen days over a dream of pleasure
Keep good wishes everything goes fine
Leave no regrets clear all doubts
Gao Shan's poem written on paper
Pray for everyone luck and happiness
Affection like rock will like iron
Feelings and thoughts connected with dreams
Peace and harmony warmer than before
Poem nearly finished sweat all over
Recall the past tears soaking shirts
Envy not wealth despise not poverty
Concord and amity precious as gold
From now on keep you company
Loving and friendly compliment much more
Gossips and affairs let them be
My old lay my dear family
Man and woman fun and pleasure
Old or young perfect pair work

Spring 2015

Dedicated to Old Yellow Flower

Wish the reunion on 3rd of lunar March all the best

黄花记事－乙未年正月廿三盛会

乙未人间太平年
正月廿三阴雨天
诗人策马入城去
单刀赴会白云边
一路风尘一路喜
昔日挚友终一起
霓裳六幺荡千里
男欢女笑乐无比
昔日少年今翁语
梦中娇颜亦老体
二十三年风和雨
曾经愁柴又愁米
今日成家且立室
看破人间无限事
逢人举酒声声思
尽酌低饮老相识
往事如烟一幕幕
曾是五楼同室住
人生轨迹多变数
虽不同道亦共路
潋能已乘黄鹤去

On Yellow Flower Gathering
3rd of lunar January 2015

A peaceful world in the year of goat
A rainy day of 3rd of lunar January
I rode to the city on my horse alone
To join a banquet at Baiyuanbian
Wind and dust all along the way
Glad to see old friends once again
Beautiful music echoed a thousand miles
Talks and laughter joy beyond comparison
Youth in the past and elderly now
Rosy faces in dream already withered
Twenty three years of wind and rain
Once a hard life with worry over food
Now successful in career and happy family
See through the many things on the earth
Raise cups to everyone feelings mixed with thoughts
Drink to my heart's content with old friends
Past experiences flash like a movie scene by scene
Once shared the same dormitory room on 5th floor
Then different paths in life with changes unavoidable
Now we are here as all roads lead to Rome
Neng deceased riding a crane to the west

锦洪不减当年红
德信歧途终送命
永润狂言省悟中
志勇曾经挥旗令
奈何今昔不两同
最爱穗雄江湖义
不偏不倚谈笑中
沛林自封谭场长
画地为山自为王
朝起摘花夜捆草
暮落观天浴野塘
粗粮淡饭能填肚
不求名利斗志昂
要数旗下谁兵多
孰人能奈场长何
一呼百应天下乱
主宰万禽生死歌
酒过半酣诗人醉
感慨人生尽蹉跎
举樽共饮邀明月
弄笔挥毫乐开怀
慧智伯乐左右立
才女宇秋铺纸开
泱泱大国逢盛世
中华儿女四海来

Jinhong is still as strong as before
Dexin went stray and it cost him his life
Yongrun talked wildly and then in meditation
Zhiyong used to be commander in the Army
But now totally different from the past
I love Huixiong best for his code of brotherhood
Righteous and justice shown in talks and laughter
Peilin called himself Manager Tan of the farm
Who plan the field and occupy it as a master
Pick flowers in the morning and bale hay at dusk
Watch the evening sky and bathe in the pond
Simple meal with coarse food grain and little meat
Pursue no fame nor fortune yet stay in high spirits
When you want to know who has more followers
Mr. Tan should be the one with no match
A hundred responses to a single call of his
Master of the many life stocks and poultry
Half through the banquet I nearly got drunk
Regret wasting so much of my life
Raised cup to the moon and drink together
Took up the writing brush joyful and free
Huizhi and Bole stood on either side
Talented lady Yuqiu helped spread the paper
To eulogize our great country at flourishing era
Sons and daughters come back from every part

华夏文明流长远
今夜更上黄花台
碧琼磨墨游偷乐
先赠杨巍后何萍
杰雄伟松齐上阵
又题何寅苏慰成
更是李宏好同志
再添子毅何道厅
言罢不见伟民影
忽闻酒仙巫忠平
戏中自有彩群舞
半途加斟百乐庭
劝君更尽一杯酒
借此紧记战友情
此起彼伏终难断
愿君借酒还独倾
宴罢筵席终须散
诗人牵马又独行
但愿来年京城见
黄花骄子天下名

2015 年春

Civilization of the Chinese Nation long and lasting
Tonight we have ascended the Yellow Flower Tower
Biqiong grinded the ink stick and You laughed secretly
First presented to Yang Wei and then He Ping
Jiexiong and Weisong came up together
Inscribed to He Yin and Su Weicheng next
Li Hong is a nice guy popular with all
With Ziyi and He Daoting to catch up with
Then Wei Min was gone nowhere to be found
Suddenly Zhongping the winebibber showed himself
Caiqun danced to add to the pleasure of gathering
Hennessy Paradis was poured half of the banquet
Please drink another cup of wine to us all
To memorize our love for friends long
As one sat down another rose hard to finish
Pour your feelings to me while drinking
Even the grandest feast must have an end
The poet rode alone on his way by horse
Hope to meet again in Beijing next year
Members of Yellow Flower known worldwide

Spring 2015

忧伤的女兵

英姿飒爽犹酣战
耿耿忠心向太阳
秋花秋叶秋不尽
那堪风雨泣凄凉
助得良庭来何速
牵愁旧梦恨离情
谁家小院无风入
何处大海无浪声
轻罗不奈寒风力
残漏岂能抗雨急
三生修来同船渡
百世方能共心齐
不知风雨何处去
已教牛郎泪窗湿

2014 年秋

Sad Women Soldiers

Valiant and heroic still in fierce fighting
Devoted to our motherland heart and soul
Autumn flowers and leaves an endless season
Weeping in solitude tortured by wind and rain
Fine houses built at home in a blink of eyes
Parting sorrow and worries remain in dream
Wind will blow into many a courtyard
Huge waves must roar in oceans and seas
Thin satin too delicate to stand the cold
Leaks and shabbiness resist no storm
Three lives of efforts make a nice couple
A thousand years will join two hearts
Wind and rain had gone before I knew it
Cowboy weeping alone wetting the curtains

Autumn 2014

春　喜

夜色朦胧寻欢去
马走羊蹄踏春来
相邀不如心默契
梦幻彷徨聚一台
才算今年谁好运
又推何日发大财
比才比艺比俊美
说东说西说胸怀
无缘隔壁难相会
好酒不请也自来
但愿羊年样样好
蝶飞凤舞百花开

2015 年春

Spring Joy

Go and seek pleasure as the night fell
The year of goat came after horse
Better unwritten understanding than appointment
Gather at the table like in a dream
Guess who will make a fortune this year
Compare talents and appearance as well
Talk about everything under the sun and feelings
Neighbors can hardly meet except by coincidence
With good wine faraway friends come by themselves
Wishing all the best for everything in the new year
Butterfly and phoenix fly over the thousand flowers

Spring 2015

忆往事

昔日花丛初识面
犹抱葵叶半遮脸
轻拈罗裙牵玉指
恨不相逢朝暮见

Recall the Past

Recalling our first meeting in the flowers
Your face half hidden behind a sunflower leaf
Lifting satin skirt and curving delicate fingers
Regret meeting late while longing to see you more

同窗寄语

折柳好花少年郎
兰麝绕身扑人香
四十不惑本该悟
奈何春心疯般狂

To My Classmate

Broke off willow twigs or admired flowers at a young age
Orchid and musk surrounded and aroma greeted the nose
Life should begin at forty with wisdom and reason
Why am I still driven insane by the desire for love

叮　嘱

莫怨情路长
缘尽倍凄凉
良宵勿虚度
玉镜淡梳妆

Extortion

Don't whine about the long way to love
More forlorn when predestined love ends
Make the best of this enjoyable night
Put on light make-up before the jade mirror

白云山

白云山上白云游，
白云悠悠小河流。
江南绿草缠幽径，
参天古树满荒丘。
飞舞珍禽日见少，
涌动人头成新忧。
总为浮云能挡月，
自然不调使人愁。

White Cloud Hill

White clouds over white cloud hill

White clouds floating like a stream flowing

Grass in south Yangtze River covers the paths

Towering old trees grow on the deserted hills

Rare birds are hardly seen in the daytime

Heads surging in crowds cause new concern

Believing floating clouds will hide the moon

Natural unbalance brings about worries to all

清华冬语

孤身北饮清华泉，
凛冽寒风衣襟巅。
飞鸟突鸣惊人语，
碎冰渐冻催虫眠。
西塘枯柳迎风立，
月下荷花隐梦间。
最爱学中求不尽，
星星之火可燎原。

Winter at Tsinghua University

Drink the Tsinghua spring water lonely
Chilly wind lifts the front of my overcoat
Flying birds sound striking like human voice
Broken ice freezes the insects into hibernation
Withered willows in west pond stand upright
Lotus flowers in moonlight drift lost in dream
My favorite is constant pursuit of knowledge
Like sparkles starting a great fire over the pasture

恨相逢

来是欢腾去无踪，
月斜醉酒五更钟。
梦为远别心难换，
思被摧残意未浓。
蜡照半空金翡翠，
麝香风雾绣芙蓉。
刘郎已恨相知晚，
更隔青山一万重。

Regret Meeting You Late

Rejoice at your coming sad about parting
At moonset we continue drinking till dawn
Dream of you far away with the same heart
Missing thought eats me lost in sadness
Candles light up half the sky appearing golden
Lotus flowers more delicate in the misty musk
My friend always regrets knowing me late
Still separated apart by a thousand mountains

春日寻梦

知己相依何处寻，
江南城外树森森。
山青水秀流春色，
隔岸鸟鸣闻好音。
十载寒窗天下闭，
蛟龙出海觅真心。
牛郎织女能相会，
独醉孤魂泪满襟。

Seek Dream on a Spring Day

Where is my bosom and reliable friend
Deep in the forest outside Jiangnan City
Beautiful landscape of mountains and rivers
Birds on the other bank are chirping sweetly
Isolated study for ten years at a cold window
A huge dragon from the sea seeks true friendship
When the Cowboy and Weaving Girl finally meet
A lonely soul will get drunk with tears over his shirt

古诗新吟

弱柳好花桃叶春，
凤皇舟上楚女群。
月华如水门初闭，
妙舞迷魂何处寻。
目送刘郎挥泪去，
两河萧瑟怨妇新。
书生怯胆车中泣，
谁梦中原沃土金？

An Old Poem Chanted in New Tune

Spring with weak willows pretty flowers peach leaves
Girls of Chu Kingdom gather on the Fenghuang boat
The moonlight flows down like a stream into the gate
Graceful dance and enchanted hearts closed inside
Seeing my friend off with tears flooding my face
Two rivers soughing like more sad women weeping
The shy scholar is sobbing alone in the carriage
Central Plains with gold like fertile soil in dream

观荷悟

绿水清香翠叶荷，
孤花自赏坠其多。
古今艳丽皆绝色，
不见貂婵笑酒窝。

Reflection on Lotus Flowers

Green lotus leaves with fragrance over clear water
Lonely flowers admiring themselves whither early
Beauties in ancient or modern times are extraordinary
Nobody's seen dimples on Diao Chan's smiling face

春　痴

缈缈云山渺渺情，
青窗绿瓦醉松鸣。
一朝坠入多情网，
千载纠缠永不清。

Infatuation With Spring

Misty mountains surrounded by cloud-like misty love
Enchanting jade windows and tiles and soughing pines
Once you fall in love as into a net woven with feelings
You will desperately be entangled here a thousand years

醉春夜

露花烟草正春深，
松密竹疏万里阴。
何事刘郎无共醉，
香残冷雨夜沾襟。

Drunk on a Spring Night

Dewy flowers misty grass in deep spring
Dense pines sparse bamboo shading miles
Liu Lang finds nobody to get drunk with
A soaked night of withered youth and cold rain

醉春风

红杏交枝映画栊，
一庭春色醉东风。
瑶池月落蝶蜂舞，
更忆芳心日夜红。

Drunk at Spring Wind

Tangled branches red apricot shaded on wood lattice
Spring scene in the courtyard enchants wind east bound
The setting moon on Heavenly Lake butterfly and bee dance
Still remember troubling over a girl's heart night and day

春　思

烟雨塘前草萋萋，
闲宵含恨堪痴迷。
惆怅春来君不见，
遥如坐梦断江溪。

Spring Fever

Misty rain moist the grass in the courtyard
Leisure night filled with hatred deserves infatuation
Depressed not at not seeing you in spring
Distant as a dream stranded by the side of a stream

春江语

柳弱蝶飞烟雨低，
千帆过尽不沾泥。
请君莫向花桥靠，
日落残莺更夜啼。

On Spring River

Willows tender butterflies flit misty rain deep

A thousand sails pass by slight and clean

Please do not lean on the flower bridge easily

At sunset only a few larks sing into the night

嫦娥醉

冰肌玉骨倍风流，
莫道娇痴不欲求。
贪与萧郎眉目语，
惊鸿竟舞错伊州。

Ecstasies Over Chang'e

Crystal skin and jade bone all the more elegant
Let alone the simple and naive that attract many
Enchanted at my lover's message sent by the eyes
Slim and graceful dance like crane as in Yi Zhou

锁春愁

泪眼桃花月色朦，
夜来潜与玉郎重。
良宵几度金丝断，
暮雨蓬莱满院空。

Sorrow Over Closed up Spring

Teary eyes peach blossoms in hazy moonlight
At night I secretly met my friend Yu Lang again
Enjoyable night once wore the spun gold out
Dusk rain echoed in empty yard like fairy land

玉楼花

泪眼桃花月色朦，
夜来潜与玉郎逢。
莺飞燕舞蝶蜂醉，
暮霭蓬莱满地红。

Flower Over Jade Tower

Teary eyes peach blossoms hazy moonlight
At night I secretly met my friend Yu Lang
Lark and swallow flying butterfly and bee enchanted
Evening mist over fairy Peng Lai dyed the land red

杏花红

楚女帘前柳万条，
愁红细雨坠平桥。
黄莺不语君何处，
轻闭朱门弄舞腰。

Apricot Trees in Bloom

Girls of Chu dance behind the curtain like a thousand willows
Flush with worries and fine rain falling over the bridge
An oriole remains silent wondering where you are going
Beauties with thin waists in the slightly shut vermillion gate

满地红

思从流水去茫茫，
一望江边烟际长。
目送征鸿飞影去，
红墙无语暗悲伤。

A Land Of Red Fallen Petals

Mind follows the river towards the misty distance
A boundless sight extending to the hazy horizon
Watch swans flying and fading in the whiteness
The red brick wall keeps silent in solitary sorrow

待郎归

夜半萧娘冷院深，
淡花瘦玉念新人。
满庭红幕垂清影，
云雨无声泪沾襟。

Expect Her Husband

At midnight a lady stays at a cold house empty
Like a pale flower or thin jade missing her husband
Her delicate profile cast on the purple curtain
Weeping at the helpless changes in the world

夜　语

舞衣红袖绣鸳鸯，
暮雨轻烟漏更长。
半敛檀眉心暗泣，
至今犹忆御炉香。

Night Whispers

Dancing red sleeves embroidered with mandarin ducks
Mist rise from dusk rain makes the night seem so long
Half-covered brows frowning the heart weeping secretly
With clear memories of the incense burner in royal palace

泪　夜

愁肠欲断翠眉低，
连理分枝芳草萋。
凭仗春风吹梦碎，
与郎终日夜东西。

Night Tears

Sorrowful heart aches and dark brows lowered
Interlocking branches and carpeting grass fragrant
Why should the spring wind break my dream half
How I would like to follow my lover night and day

惆　怅

满院残红冷露伤，
朱唇未动雪腮香。
琵琶半抱别君曲，
不忍心愁万里郎。

Grief

Fallen petals carpet the courtyard frosted in cold dew
Red lips shut and fair cheeks scented with aroma
Farewell music played on a Chinese lute half hidden
Worrying about her lover ten thousands miles away

连珠妙语

一舟碧浪千山过，
两岸猿声滚滚来。
三面环山烟没雨，
四朋赏景上高台。
五层登尽文阁顶，
六步吟诗门自开。
七弄琵琶出梦语，
八听绿水荡秋怀。
九天落幕银河觅，
十载寒窗遇怪才。

Witty Remarks Like A String Of Pearls

A white sail on blue sea passed a thousand miles
Apes howling endlessly along both banks
Mist and rain overlap mountains on three sides
Four friends admire scenery on a high terrace
Five flights of stairs lead to the top of a pagoda
A poem is completed while walking six steps
Seven times the lute is played on lyrics in dream
Eight trips to the river to show my feeling of autumn
The Ninth Heaven curtains fall lost in the Milky Way
Ten years'study by cold window met an eccentric talent

白玉盆

箭逐鸿落坠，
鹰觅月环飞。
寿献金桃露，
莺歌白鹭肥。
舟浮溪吐月，
亭映夜波辉。
月入闺门静，
人闲月不归。

White Jade Plate

Arrows falling with the geese

Hawks flying around the moon

Golden peach wine presented for longevity

Larks singing while aigrettes eating contented

The moon rises from behind the floating boat

Pavilions reflect on glowing lake at night

Moonlight slips into a lady's quiet gate

The moon lingers in the sky like men at leisure

醉芙蓉

永夜刘郎何处去，
香阁轻掩断来音。
月沉花好香犹在，
弱柳小庭怨误衾。
换我佳期成病忍，
谁家寂寂翠箔深。
莺啼燕语弦清越，
惹恨缠绵碎夜襟。

Lotus Flowers Enchanted at Night

Where has her husband gone for the long night
Her scented house slightly shut from messages
The moon set   fragrance of blossoms lingers
Weak willows in small yard whine of late return
My otherwise enjoyable night is but a painful wait
Can you find other green curtains as silent as mine
Larks and swallows sing like clear beautiful music
Tears of self-asked sentiments wrinkle my dress

袅垂杨

小桃细雨弄罗裳，
舞燕飞花万点妆。
芳草梧桐春梦醒，
斜阳满地觅遗香。

Tender Willows

Peach buds and fine rain moist the silk dress
Dancing swallows swirling flowers dotted
Grass and Lakka trees awake from spring dream
The sunset glow looks for left scent over the land

倾花酒

月沉银河静，
人悄赏海棠。
莺啼沙鹭去，
绿蚁醉红妆。

Wine Poured by Pretty Girls

The sky quiets down at moonset
Admire crabapple blossoms alone
Larks sing and ospreys flit by
Girls drunk with new-brewed wine

离　别

握手河桥泪滥襟，
蜂须惹尽百花心。
楚烟湘月皆沉落，
欲语难言寄翠琴。

Parting

Wave goodbye on the bridge tears soaked the shirt
Bees flit from one stamen to another flowers troubled
Smoke from Chu and moonlight in Xiang both descend
Feelings in hesitation are expressed by playing the lute

渡愁云

羞红鬓浅恨残云，
片片花蕊点绿茵。
燕尾分离千怨毕，
宝驱弃勒万疆轻。
尘波带雨题门外，
玉背婀娜渡楚身。
惆怅幽期庭树冷，
寒暄不致念无痕。

Clouds Heavy With Gloom

Flush in cheeks quiet whine like pale cloud
Green grass dotted with delicate petals
Swallow lines parted all complaints end
Fine horses rejected the reins and traveled light
Dusty rain left stains on the gate like inscriptions
Girls from Chu dance with slim jade-like figures
As trees in the courtyard shiver in long sorrow
Wonder where they are with no letters of greetings

闲　春

长安古道马嘶嘶，
目断夕阳鸟去时。
绿酒生疏人散尽，
春风早过少年期。

Leisurely Spring

On Chang'an ancient paths horse neigh
The setting sun fades and birds flew away
Guests disperse when the wine is finished
The spring wind has already passed its youth

风雨云丝

天边菊紫露成霜，
日夜愁云莫断肠。
欲醉清歌空对酒，
飞鸿过尽惹君伤。

Slanting Rain and Gossamer Cloud

Violet glow along the horizon dews frost
Sorrowful days and nights break the heart
To sing while drinking and get myself drunk
Swans flow past leaving you in sadness long

离 愁

伤高怀远最情浓，
无语濛濛飞絮重。
嘶骑随尘芳草乱，
双鸳戏舞水溶溶。
梯横倩影黄昏后，
斜月帘栊梦境中。
细恨沉量思几度，
不如桃杏嫁东风。

Grief of Parting

Deepest is the missing thought of one far away
Keeping silent staring at the misty willow catkins
Horses neighing raising dust disturbing the grass
Mandarin ducks tumbling water in merry harmony
Ladder cast shadow after dusk near the house
Setting moon out of the window emerges in dream
Complaints and worries keep mingled and overlapped
Better follow east wind like peach and apricot blossoms

双红醉

隐隐林间鸟，
幽幽九里香。
双红出绿叶，
恰似睡鸳鸯。

Two Pretty Petals

Birds hidden in the distant woods
Camunings in the misty distance
Two petals against the green leaves
Like two mandarin ducks in sleep

念春愁

草绿荒丘尽，
桃红倒影长。
时时思旧事，
每每更心伤。
闭目闻啼鸟，
清心享野香。
春从流水去，
还我绿衣裳。

Hidden Bitterness In Spring

Green grass extends to the end of highland
Peach blossoms reflect on the ground long
Now and then I can’t help thinking of the past
Always drown myself in helpless sadness
Closing my eyes there come the birds chirping
Enjoy the fragrance of the wild peacefully
Spring is gone with the flowing current
Please give me back my green dress to keep

忆江南

独有碎情人，
偏亲草木春。
银轮出海浅，
翠柳渡江轻。
莺舞随歌去，
忧痴近我身。
不堪鬓眷泪，
来对苦眠吟。

Recall The South

Such a lonely lover I am
Attached to the spring trees
The moon rises above the seashore
Young willows across the river light
Larks dance disappear with the music
Leaving sorrow and infatuation with me
Can't hold back tears rolling down cheeks
But write a poem when sleep comes hard

翠娥愁

修蛾慢脸锁云鬟，
纤手罗衣绿蚁昏。
心荡思云无睡意，
身归念雨有愁痕。
莺啼蝶舞春吹室，
细雨桃花梦醒魂。
谁见夕阳孤梦乐，
独林带冷粉泪温。

Sad Pretty Girl

A clean-cut face lined with dark hair
Delicate hands satin dress new brewed wine
Her heart floats like cloud with no sense of sleep
Get back still missing the rain mixed with grief
Lark sing butterfly dance spring fills the house
Fine rain peach blossom a lonely soul awake
Who knows the setting sun happy in dream alone
Only the woods sees powered tears still warm

忆

深山高不测，
幽处现孤云。
枫隙出新月，
花间隐鹤群。
清光寻古寺，
静夜觅凄君。
惆怅东方处，
西山忆苦音。

Recall

Hidden mountain with height hard to measure
A lonely cloud emerged from the depth
Between maple trees rises the crescent moon
While cranes dance behind the flowers
Seek ancient temple in morning light
Find my miserable friend on a quiet night
Rather leave sorrows lingering in the east
Than recall sad messages from the west

寻月夜曲

青山碧水白云间，
绿蚁清琴夜未眠。
淡荡逍遥逢浅志，
寻思往事月遮天。

Seek Nocturne in Moonlight

Green mountains blue rivers white clouds
New brewed wine clear flute sleepless night
Wander about at leisure my incomplete will
Think of the past the moon overspreads the sky

再别茶溪谷

轻轻的我来了
正如你轻轻的走
我轻轻的招手
作别昨天的沉默
那茶溪的暮谷
是夕阳中的新郎
波光里的倩影
在我的心头飘过
春湖上的黑鹅
柔柔的在云底招摇
在茶溪的秋波里
我甘心做一叶孤舟
那梧荫下的一片
不是嫩绿
是天上嫦娥
沉醉在溪沟
宁静着蔷薇似的梦
寻梦？拐一支长矛
向花蕊更深处漫溯
满载一夜星辉
在星辉斑斓里沉沦

Farewell to Chaxi Valley

So quietly I come here
As quietly as you left
Quietly I wave my hand
Farewell to the silence of yesterday
The valley of Chaxi in the dusk
Is the bridegroom in the setting sun
The delicate reflection on the stream
Flit across my heart slightly
Black swans on the spring lake
Softly swaying under the clouds
In the ripples of Chaxi Stream
I'm willing to be a lonely boat
The little patch of shade below a parasol tree
Is not tinted with fresh green
But the fairy Chang'e in the Moon Palace
Who is immersed in the valley
Peaceful in his rose like dream
To seek dream just take a spear
Point to the depth of the blossoms
Fully loaded with stars glowing
Sink into the splendor of starry night

但我不能沉沦
悄悄是别离的长篙
野马也为我沉默
沉默是今晚的茶谷
悄悄的我来了
正如你悄悄的走
我挥一挥心絮
散落是遍地的云霞

2015年春

But I can not sink myself now

Quietly is the departure of a rowing boat

A wild horse keeps silent for me as well

Silent tonight is also the Chaxi Valley

So quietly I come here

As quietly as you left

I wave my pack of mixed feelings

Like the rosy clouds scattering on the ground

Spring 2015

断 章

我在檐下看手掌
看手掌的人在湖边等我
不知道是手机里的人在找我
还是我在找找手机的人
世界有时乱得
连你都不知道
还好意思来问我

2015 年春

Fragments

I watch my palm below the eave
The one watching his palm is expecting me by the lake
Whether the one in the mobile phone is looking for me
Or I am looking for him
The world is at times disorderly so
If you don't know it yourself
Why should you bother to ask me

Spring 2015-5-20

茶溪春语

夜宿华侨城
朝闻百鸟声
踏歌茶溪谷
湖畔野鸭惊

2015 年春

On Spring of Chaxi

Stay over night at Ocean Seas Chinese City
Hear hundreds of birds chirping in the morning
Walk through Chaxi Valley singing all the way
Startling the wild ducks on both sides of the lake

Spring 2015

新好了歌

世人都晓神仙好，惟有股票忘不了！
中外牛市在何方？破产重组钱没了！
世人都晓神仙好，只有房产忘不了！
砸锅卖铁买不够，及到多时暴跌了。
世人都晓神仙好，只有移民忘不了！
倾家荡产到国外，最后条条回来了！
世人都晓神仙好，只有存折忘不了！
通货膨胀古来多，钞机一开贬值了！
世人都晓神仙好，只有淑女忘不了！
朝三暮四喜沾沾，精疲力尽人垮了！
世人都晓神仙好，只有美酒忘不了！
对酒当歌问几何，一醉方休不活了！

2015 年春

New Version of a Song With a Good Ending

Everyone admires immortals but attached to stock shares
Seek profitable market? Bankrupt, reorganize and money gone
Admire immortals but hold on to houses and properties
Sell furniture and cookery to buy real estate then sudden loss
Admire the immortals but longing to immigrate abroad
Dissipate all fortune to go abroad and return empty handed
Admire the immortals but keep the bank account books
Inflation happens often and money devalue at bill counter
Admire immortals but keep chasing fair ladies
Excited at dawn three and dusk four, exhausted and down
Admire immortals but addicted to wine and grand feast
Sing while drinking and get drunk forgetting everything

Spring 2015

忘了歌

世人都晓传统好，惟有仁爱忘记了！
寻贵问贱求出身，囊中羞涩免谈了！
世人都晓传统好，只有礼义忘记了！
己所不欲又施人，恃强凌弱不得了！
世人都晓传统好，只有智信忘记了！
不学无术如走尸，一言既出不算了！
世人都晓传统好，只有孝悌忘记了！
父母兄弟又如何，抛妻弃子人去了！

2015 年春

Let It Go

Praise fine tradition but forget kindness /benevolence
Concern about family background despise the penniless
Praise promote fine tradition but neglect etiquette
Do to others what one avoids and bully the weak madly
Promote fine tradition but ignore wisdom and fidelity
Lack in knowledge and ability and fail to keep promise
Promote fine tradition but filial piety and fraternity missing
Desert wife and kids, let alone one's parents and siblings

Spring 2015

梦 语

昨夜辗转眠
今朝呓语间
日日忙碌碌
不光为银元
先获人赞赏
后把己欲填
教人应几许
便是心坎言
瘦蛙鸣井底
猛龙腾苍天
估算须远见
举步当超前
将人先比己
便知律千篇
欲穷万壑景
更上泰山巅
近朱先己赤
临墨定易黑
心宽能体胖
志短必将悲
勤劳终致富

Dream Words

Restless in sleep last night
Talking like in dream this morning
Kept busy night and day
Not just for cash and money
First for praise and honor
Then to satisfy own's desire
Teach morals and disciplines
Al from the bottom of my heart
Thin frogs crack in the well
Fierce dragons fly in the sky
Foresee the far future
Take steps in advance
Put myself in others' place
Know the natural law much
See the sights through the valleys
Ascend to the top of Mountain Tai
Behave myself to be with the well behaved
Hold the writing brush steadily and well
A sound mind consists in a sound body
A weak will surely lead to a sad end
Hard work brings about good wealth

懈懒老来贫
教子须从早
爱妻鉴古今
求财非难事
套路自应新
诚信心扉烙
迎合最当真
家和万事好
邻安比千金
闻鸡应起舞
劝君日日勤
心中无难事
举重便若轻
岁月莫蹉跎
年日更如歌
往来皆君子
不妨多切磋
荣辱能与共
常思常琢磨
闲暇开书卷
无事学丘轲
兄弟同根树
佩剑莫相磨
人成己亦喜
他伤泪滂沱

Laziness must result in poor old age
Children education should starts early
Love one's wife and follow the tradition
Not so difficult to earn a fortune
Seek new ways to achieve your goal
Always bear credibility in mind
Show sincerity to each other
A peaceful family will prosper
Safe neighbours valuable as old
Rise early as the cock start crowing
Better be diligent day to day
Consider nothing to be difficult
Handle everything with ease
Never waste any minute
Years go like a river flowing
Get along with refined people
Exchange and communicate more
Share joy and sorrow with each other
Reflect and meditate constantly
Read a lot whenever having time
Always learn from Confucius and Mencius
Brothers are from the same family tree
Never should we pull sword at each other
Happy for others' success
Sad at others' misfortune

纵有百般过
不可挥干戈
寒蚓生松土
巨蟒出嵯峨
心存凌云志
无人奈你何
就此先收笔
愿君悟更多

2015 年春

Even with a hundred faults
Not enough to cost one's life
Winter worms live in loose soil
Giant pythons survive from hard rock
With a high aim in mind
Nobody can defeat you
End the verse with this sentence
Wish you more understanding of life

Spring 2015

松花霁雪

松花雪霁白山头
玉树红霞绿壑沟
愿与嫦娥常醉月
千杯难解恨中愁

Pine Pollens After Snow

Pine pollens after snow on white capped mountain
Evening glow over jade trees down the green valley
Wish to get drunk on the moon with fairy Chang'e
A thousand cups of wine can't relieve my sadness

郊野鸣

朽木新枝惹鸟啼
邀朋醉死北江西
春风不解牛郎意
莫待秋还泪满溪

Birds Chirping in The Wild

Birds chirp at new twigs from dead wood
Drown in wine with friends west to North River
Spring wind fails to follow Cow Boy's heart
Don't wait till autumn fills the stream with tears

欲望之殇

嘭嘭的脚步
踏落了一地砖瓦
振碎了千里河山
以掩耳盗铃之势
暗流汹涌
浊浪澎湃

欲望之徒
挥舞着长矛短剑
根深蒂固
欲火中烧、磨拳擦掌
满脸横肉、杀气腾腾

砰砰的心跳
有如大海咆哮
狂风的怒号
吓坏了山川湖海
渺茫消沉
颓丧乏味

End of Desire

Pounding footsteps
Breaking the tiles and bricks
Shaking the mountains and rivers
Come down like a thunder
Undercurrent rolling
Turbid surging

Embodiment of desire
Waves his spear and sword
Deeply rooted
Desire is burning rub his fists and wipe his palms
Cross-grained featured   threatening

Pounding heart
Roaring like the sea
Howling like a gale
Frightening the mountains and rivers
Falling   receding
Dull in the dumps

一座座高耸的楼房
如雨后初笋
参差错落、高低不一
一条条笔直的铁道
东南西北、长短不齐
还有、那些财囊、珠宝
以及、那些裙子、舞郎

欲望张开血盆大口
不假思索
逐一吞噬
片甲不留

继续、继续
挥动着巨臂、盆开海口
喷发出魔鬼般的欲火
青蓝黄绿
所向披靡
遍地嚎伤

转而
万物复苏、燕子归南
百鸟争鸣、蝶蜂绕栏
初春的气息淹没了
阴阳怪气

High rises one by one
Spring up like bamboo sprouts
Irregular   tall or short
Rails one after another
Stretch in all directions   long or short
And all the treasures   jewelry
And all the skirts   dancing boys

The Desire opens his bloody mouth
Without thinking
Swallows the all
Leaving not a bit

Continue   continue
Waving his giant arm open his mouth
Blow evil flames
Balck   blue   yellow   green
Make a clean sweep of all obstacles along his path
Deaths and wounds scattered

Then
Everything awakes   swallows fly back to the south
All birds chirp   butterflies and bees hover around
Early spring has conquered the ghosts and monsters
Fresh breeze smoothers the embodiment of desire

初醒的微风吹熄了
欲望之狂

梦寐的春雨
柳绿枝扬、霏霏蒙蒙
晨光熹微
逐而亮白出万丈光芒
光芒四射、照耀出
壮丽的初生
初生之犊、收复了平衡
抚摸温柔着昨日的沧桑
平息了波澜
消亡了欲狂

远远望去、不远处
那欲望之火慢慢消散
消散出一片坦然
坦然的天空、宽广蔚蓝
天空之下、是多情的大地
大地上、我发现了
丘轲在交谈！从此！
不再惊慌！！

2015年春

Dream spring rain falls
Willows extend their branches   in green mist
Morning glow
Shines in all its splendor through the mist
Radiate glories over everything fresh
The new born calf   recover
Stroke tenderly the past wounds
Put down the troubles
Terminate the ebodiment of desire

Looking into the distance
Flames of desire die down   disperse
Leaving a stretch of calmness
Calm sky   the vast azure
With the affectionate land below
On which I find Confucius and Mencius are talking
From now on there will be
No more panic and fright

Spring 2015

秋　伤

昨夜琼楼梦
今宵旷野吟
孤鹏飞大海
双鸳聚丛林
月本无圆缺
情自有浅深
汉南秋瑟瑟
焉得不凄心

2014 年秋

Sorrow in Autumn

Dream of heavenly house last night
Chant poems on the vast plain today
Lonely roc soaring over the ocean
Mandarin ducks gather in the forest
The moon remains itself whether full or wane
Only passion can become deep or shallow
Autumn bleak and rustling in south of Han
How can I not be shivering at heart now

Autumn 2014

秋 吟

凡躯寿有限
慧思命无穷
昨夜梨花梦
晨阳付东风
几处红叶落
谁家白帘栊
最是离恨重
南北一般同

2014 年秋

A Poem on Autumn

Mortals are granted limited lives
But wise thoughts will last long
Dream of pear blossoms yesterday
All gone with east wind this morning
Maple leaves fallen in a few places
Whose white curtain sills decorated
Saddest is the sorrow of parting
Whether in the south or the north

Autumn 2014

无眠夜曲

庭深长夜静
来世共婵娟
红烛秋初倦
绿席夜未眠
凭栏拂杂念
倚石去愁烟
同饮一江水
天翁应解怜

2014 年秋

Sleepless Night

Quiet night seems long in empty yard
Admire the moon together next life
Red candle weary in early autumn
Sleepless night on green bamboo sheet
Lean against railing and clear all troubles
Rest on the rock helps forget all worries
We all fetch water from the same river
Heaven should show sympathy on us

Autumn 2014

寒　月

深秋寒月西窗静
点点凝珠恨难平
红烛半消逢夜短
枕前无事最伤情

2014 年秋

The Chilly Moon

Deep autumn chilly moon outside quiet west windows
Tears drops freeze on my checks and my troubled heart
Red candles half burnt seem especially short at night
Nothingness on the pillow shows a depressed mood

Autumn 2014

仙女记

灵丹妙药天山栽
冰肌玉骨人间来
乱入人群看不见
闻声国学百花开

2014 年秋

To Fairy

Elixir grows in the heavenly mountain only
Beauty of flesh of ice and bones of jade descends to earth
Once mingled in the crowd nowhere to be seen
Reading Chinese classics like various flowers in full bloom

Autumn 2014

人　生

莫怨苦路长
离合伤别促
遥途丰有余
晨晓欢不足
我若西流水
君为东岱岳
慷慨言国学
憔悴就童育
安得彩云里
梦幻成驯服

2014 年秋

Life

Complain not about long hardship
Parting and sorrow can be instant
Journey to the distance always endless
Happy hours never seem enough
I am like a river simply flowing west
You are high and lofty like Mount Tai
Present your ideas on sinology eloquently
Devoted to education thin and pallid
Wish to stay in the colorful clouds
Dreams are tame horses under control

Autumn 2014

世事难

人间世事样样难
东风无力百花残
囊中羞涩三江白
霜清纸帐五更寒
绿蓑舟上秋闻笛
鹦鹉楼头夜倚栏
醉酹刘伶应自问
何缘牛织不团圆

2014 年秋

Hard World

Everything may be hard in the world
East wind can't save flowers from withering
Short of money and everywhere looks bleak
Frosty night the thin curtain feels cold
On green straw caped boat flute is heard
By Parrot Tower I lean against the railing
Sage of the Bamboo Grove Liu Ling should ask himself
Why can't Cowboy and Weaving Girl be reunited

Autumn 2014

无难事

都说世事难
梦醒情何堪
尽兴常思玩
牵愁不忍观
世间无难事
只怕有心人
牛织隔南北
天下最知音
悲观不可取
坚强贵比金
孤木方可朽
三树便成林
热酒迎宾客
香茶对友人
无事篱畔坐
有感抱膝吟
炎黄多名著
千古风流人
建功勤立业
救苦助红尘
孝敬老长辈

No Hard Times

Hard times in the world talked about
The waking hours are hard to bear
Often enjoy myself fully at leisure
Avoid seeing the sad and cruel reality
But where there is a will
There should be a way as they say
Cowbody and Weaving Girl set apart
With their hearts joint all the time
Never adopt a pessimistic attitude
Being strong and tough values more
A lonely tree may get rotten easily
Three trees will surely make a grove
Welcome my guests with warm wine
Treat my old friends to the finest tea
Enjoy sitting by the hedge at leisure
Chant a poem myself when touched
So many classics in Chinese history
So many talents in the past years
Make achievements and success in career
Extend a helping hand to the needed
Respect and care for the elderly

天下父母亲
春光休辜负
桃园惜寸阴
只要功夫深
铁杵磨成针
有缘千里会
无情独拥衾
苦尽甘来伴
你我最欢心
弄笔何人墨
江南高山文

2014 年秋

Parents are our dearest in the world
Never waste youthful hours
Seize the minute and second of life
As long as you work hard enough
You can grind an iron rod into a needle
Fate will bring us together from miles away
Indifference will leave one alone in bed
Sweetness comes after bitterness for old couple
We are both filled with happiness again
Who is waving his writing brush in excitement
It is poet Gao Shan from south of Yangtze River

Autumn 2014

国　学

昨日谈大学
今宵论中庸
儒家说治国
道教言无穷
四海皆兄弟
北大聚英雄
沧桑已历尽
焉得夜匆匆
推心置腹后
天下太平中
孤木朽荒野
万花遍山红
人生皆如梦
何不醉朦胧

2014 年秋
北大

Sinology

Talked about The Great Learning yesterday
Discuss on The Doctrine of Mean today
The Confucians managing state affairs
Daoists believing the infinitude of the world
Within the four seas all men are brothers
Heroes now gather in Beijing University
Going through all turbulent times in life
How can the night pass in such an instant
After expressing our feelings and thoughts
The world seems to lie in complete peace
Lonely wood may be left rotten in the wild
Thousands of flowers in bloom over the hills
Human life is all but a dream and illusion
Why not drink and remain in cloudiness

Autumn 2014
Beijing University

大　学

大学之道道明德
亲民至善言不阿
知止且定后能静
能安能虑后能得
事有始终物本末
知所先后得益多
格物致知且诚意
推己及人先正心
修身齐家且治国
自此方能平天下
国学大道数不尽
天子庶人应入心
自强不息行大道
天下为公日日勤
言而必行行必果
坦诚相待甚比金
互仁互爱互相让
国学精粹益古今
从你从我从他起
从此天涯若比邻

2014年秋
北大

The Great Learning

The Great Learning is all about wisdom and virtue
Being amicable and kind with refined language
Know how to stop and calm down in a peaceful mind
Rest and consider so as to have a grasp of everything
Everything has beginning and ending in the right order
Put priority to things and weighing thus benefit gained
Study the nature to acquire knowledge with sincerity
Consider others in my own place with a righteous heart
Cultivate myself regulate family and manage the state
In order to maintain the peace of the whole world
Doctrines of Chinese classics are all comprehensive
Whether emperor or ordinary people keep them in mind
Exert myself constantly and follow the Great Course
A public spirit rules all under the sky working hard daily
Be truthful in deed and firm in action over everything
Treating each other frankly is worth more than gold
Be kindhearted and gentle and love each other
Essence of Chinese classics influential and lasting
Begin from ourselves and carry out these doctrines
Thousands miles away seems like next door neighbor

Autumn 2014
Beijing University

念

善恶一念间
梦醒半床前
昨夜惊古刹
今朝悟千年
上山观白虎
下海觅龙虔
天涯皆咫尺
知音远无边

2014 年秋
北大

Thoughts

Only one thought between good and evil
Half awake I am from dream lying in bed
Shocked at the sight of ancient temple last night
Understand history thousands of years today
Watch white tigers on top of the mountain
Seek dragon down the depth of the ocean
Edge of the world can be an inch nearby
The bosom friend still seems miles away

Autumn 2014
Beijing University

中华七字歌

华夏善如水
炎黄子孙同
高风亮节处
千古立场中
齐家治国志
凡事应中庸
仁义道德孝
国兴万家和
欲问何所悟
中华古诗歌
欲问孰最懂
悠悠九州河

2014 年秋
北大

Song To The Chinese Nation

Greatest benevolence of Chinese is like water
Descendents of the Yan and Huang Emperors
With exemplary conduct and noble character
Stick to righteousness and justice forever
Determination to regulate family and manage state
Follow the Doctrines of Mean managing everything
Humanity justice   propriety morality and filial piety
Family peace and comfort depend on country prosperity
How do you understand the above principles
Chinese classical poems are constantly admired
Who understands best all over the world
The rivers ever flowing with a distant source

Autumn 2014
Beijing University

念郎归

孤庙寒潮雨萧萧
谢娘惆怅泪千条
暮天听愁思悲乐
刘郎何处静悄悄

2014 年秋

Expecting Her Husband

An isolated temple with cold rain rustling in
A lady is weeping sad tears soaking her dress
Listen to the sorrowful music lost in thought
Where has her husband gone leaving no message

Autumn 2014